Instructor's Handbook
to accompany

Lives and Moments

AN INTRODUCTION TO SHORT FICTION

Hans Ostrom
University of Puget Sound

Holt, Rinehart and Winston, Inc.

Fort Worth   Chicago   San Francisco   Philadelphia
Montreal   Toronto   London   Sydney   Tokyo

ISBN: 0-03-030377-X

Address Editorial Correspondence To:	301 Commerce, Suite 3700 Fort Worth, TX 76102
Address Orders To:	6277 Sea Harbor Drive Orlando, FL 32887 1-800-782-4479, or 1-800-433-0001 (in Florida)

Printed in the United States of America

0 1 2 3 095 9 8 7 6 5 4 3 2 1

Holt, Rinehart and Winston, Inc.
The Dryden Press
Saunders College Publishing

CONTENTS

1. Videotapes and Films for Teaching the Short Story

About the Short Story

"What Is A Short Story? A Discussion By Clifton Fadiman"; 14 minutes. Distributed by Kent State Video and Film Rental Center.

"The Short Story"; 48 minutes. (Includes material on stories by O. Henry, Flannery O'Connor, and Jean Stafford.) Distributed by Center for the Humanities.

Individual Authors

(Interviews, dramatizations of short stories, etc.)

Alice Adams. Interview; 49 minutes. Distributed by American Audio Prose Library Series.

Toni Cade Bambara. Interview; 58 minutes. Distributed by American Audio Prose Library Series.

Ann Beattie. Interview; 57 minutes. Distributed by American Audio Prose Library Series.

Raymond Carver. Interview; 51 minutes. Distributed by American Audio Prose Library Series.

Anton Chekhov. "A Writer's Life"; 37 minutes. Distributed by Films for the Humanities.

Arthur Conan Doyle. "The Adventure of the Speckled Band"; 58 minutes. (Starring Jeremy Brett and David Burke. Originally on PBS.) Distributed by Simon and Schuster Communications.

William Faulkner. "Barn Burning"; 41 minutes. (Starring Tommy Lee Jones and Sharon Whittington.) Distributed by Center for the Humanities.

Nathaniel Hawthorne. "A Biography of Nathaniel Hawthorne";23 minutes. Distributed by International Film Bureau.

Ernest Hemingway. "Grace Under Pressure"; (biographical) 57 minutes. Distributed by Films for the Humanities.

Ernest Hemingway. "Hemingway"; 60 minutes. (Starring Rob Townsend.) Distributed by Idaho State University.

Henry James. "Henry James"; (biographical) 23 minutes. Distributed by Journal Films.

James Joyce. "James Joyce"; (documentary) 80 minutes. Distributed by Films for the Humanities.

James Joyce. "**The Dead**"; (dramatization); 83 minutes. (Starring Anjelica Huston and Donald McCann.) Distributed by Vestron Pictures.

Franz Kafka. "**The Trials of Franz Kafka**" (biographical); 154 minutes. Distributed by Films for the Humanities.

D.H. Lawrence. "**D.H. Lawrence**" (biographical); 30 minutes. Distributed by Best Films.

Herman Melville. "**Bartleby**" (dramatization); 28 minutes. Distributed by Kent State Video and Film Rental Center.

Herman Melville. "**American Gothic: Hawthorne/Melville**"; 28 minutes. Distributed by Center for the Humanities.

Edgar Allan Poe. "**The Literature of Melancholy**" (biographical); 30 minutes. Distributed by Center for the Humanities.

Edgar Allan Poe. "**A Visit With The Author**"; 30 minutes. (Includes reading of "The Tell-Tale Heart.") Distributed by Perennial Education.

John Updike. Interview; 28 minutes. Distributed by American Audio Prose Library Series.

Alice Walker. Interview; 45 minutes. Distributed by American Audio Prose Library Series.

Eudora Welty. "**On Storytelling**"; 53 minutes. Distributed by American Audio Prose Library Series.

2. Guidelines for Group Work in Creative Writing

[Note to instructors: The audience for these guidelines is the students.]

It's a good idea for groups to "warm up" before they begin the real work. Even introducing yourself will break the ice. Consult the instructor for lengthier warm-up exercises. The most important feature of group work is common respect combined with common effort. You are a team. You are under no obligation to be friends, but you are obligated to respect one another. Keep the focus of discussion on the writing, not the writer.

1. Distribute copies of your story, and, if you like, say a few words about it, but not many. In particular, don't make excuses. Have the story photocopied and collated before you come to class.

2. Read the story aloud—slowly enough to project a sense of your prose rhythm. Do not read too fast. Anytime you stumble, circle the word or passage, especially with dialogue.

3. The listeners should mark troublesome words, sentences, or sections as the author reads, but not in a way that will distract the author. Listen hard and be respectful.

4. After the author reads, everyone will *write* a brief response, either on the back of the story or on a separate sheet. At this point, the author may either write his/her own response or go get a drink of water; at first this silence can be disconcerting.

Limit the writing period to five to seven minutes. Concentrate on larger elements (character, conflict, key scenes, etc.). Do not nit pick. Spelling and typos are not important at this stage because the instructor will read the story carefully later and make comments about these.

5. In the discussion, the author must remain silent, except to answer informational questions, which should be rare. The silence will be difficult at first, but it is absolutely essential. Do not start explaining or defending the story. What you want to find out is how the story "struck" the group. Your story needs no defense; it automatically has worth.

Because the author is silent, the other group members must be courteous and fair in their comments. When it is your turn to comment, start by saying what you liked about the story and then move on to other comments. Stick to the larger elements. Never be sarcastic. Never make fun of anyone's writing.

Suggestion: Resist the urge to rewrite the story for the author. Instead of saying, for example, "You ought to have the character start yelling here," stress the way in which the existing scene struck you. Let the author decide what changes to make.

6. Will group members disagree about a story? Of course! But remember, disagreements need not be resolved. All you need to do is to make any disagreements clear to the author; then he or she can decide whom to believe. You do not need to draw out debates. Just state positions.

7. After everyone has spoken, the author may ask one or two questions for clarification, but the author should not explain or defend the story or any part of it.

5

8. After you have read your story, always come to class for subsequent readings. Group work depends on equal effort.

3. Guidelines for In-Class Evaluation of Drafts of Essays on Short Stories

[Note to instructors: Peer evaluation can be helpful in a variety of ways. It provides students with a real audience for their work-in-progress, it shows them how another writer approached the assignment, it reinforces the idea of revision, and it stresses the connection between critical thinking and writing. Having students <u>write</u> a response to a draft is crucial because it makes the response pointed and detailed and because it allows the instructor to shape the general nature of the response without telling students exactly what to say. Peer evaluation also avoids the problem of students believing that they are writing only for the teacher. The following guidelines are for pairs of students working on drafts, but they could be adapted to groups of three or four or more.]

A. Summarize the thesis of your essay in one or two sentences.

B. In a paragraph, describe the one or two major difficulties you are now having at this stage of writing your essay.

C. Exchange the responses to A and B and your draft with your partner, and read the responses and draft.

D. After you have finished reading, *write* a response to the following:

    1. How clear is the thesis? In what ways might the author qualify or revise the thesis?

    2. Are there places where you wanted more explanation of or evidence for the author's point of view? Explain.

3. Describe one additional strength and one additional weakness of your partner's draft.

E. After each of you has written the responses, discuss one another's drafts. Do not merely exchange your written responses; explain them and elaborate on them.

F. After the discussion, take a few minutes to make notes about how you want to change your draft.

4. Guidelines for In-Class Evaluation of Drafts of Short Stories

A. Exchange drafts of the stories with your partner and read each draft twice.

B. Write a response to the following:

1. How typical and how individual is the main character? To what extent do we need more particular, significant detail about the character? Explain.

2. In the pages you have read so far, how clearly is the conflict developed? What about the conflict is unclear to you now?

3. List three memorable images from the draft.

C. After each of you has written responses, discuss the rough drafts. Do not merely exchange the responses; explain them and elaborate on them.

D. Write or revise for 15 minutes.

5. Guidelines for Interpreting Short Stories in a Group

Divide the class into groups of three, four, or five. Give them the following directions (or write them on the board).

A. In your group, take turns reading a paragraph of the story out loud until you have finished reading the story.

B. Individually, write a monologue (one-half page) spoken by any secondary character in the story (Queenie, Lengel, "the witch," Stokesie, etc.). In this monologue give "your" (your character's) point of view on what Sammy does. For example, if you choose Lengel, explain what you think of Sammy and of what Sammy chose to do.

C. Take turns reading these monologues out loud.

The instructor can visit groups during the readings, asking students why they had their characters say certain things. After the readings, the instructor can reconvene the class for a general discussion of the story, if there is time.

6. Twelve Additional Collaborative Activities for the Classroom

Collaborative activities promote active learning on the part of students. They also give more reserved students an opportunity to contribute their ideas, and they can energize a class by altering the pattern of lecture and lecture/discussion and by removing the instructor from "the center" of the classroom.

I have used all of the exercises (or variations thereof) either in Prelude —a writing-and-thinking workshop for entering freshmen that the University of Puget Sound offers before classes begin each fall—or in a sophomore-level creative writing class. The creative writing class is in the core curriculum, so it also serves as an introduction to short fiction and includes literary analysis as well as the students' own creative work. I have also used similar exercises in freshman-writing courses and other kinds of writing and literature courses. I am indebted to many colleagues at Puget Sound with whom I have exchanged ideas about collaborative learning

1. Divide the class into groups of three to five students and have them develop an approach to adapting a short story to a film. What visual qualities in the short story would they emphasize? What scene would they choose to begin the film? How would they cast the film? To make the exercise briefer, one might have them discuss only one scene in a short story.

A recorder in the group should write down the groups's decisions, and then report to the class as a whole. The instructor can lead the way in comparing and contrasting the film versions, and in encouraging the students to discuss how these versions enhanced their sense of the short story.

Purpose: This exercise allows students to focus on imagery, to see a short story as a group of scenes, and to approach conflict and character from a cinematic angle. The exercise also makes use of their "cinematic literacy." The exercise can be used after the class has actually viewed a film version of a short story. Also, the exercise is probably more useful after the basic vocabulary of literary interpretation has been introduced.

2. Divide the class into pairs, and have the pairs review several stories that the class has read and list the points of view in which these stories were written. (If there is an odd number of students, the instructor may create one trio or join in to form another pair.) As the pairs work on this information, they will inevitably have to clarify between themselves what "first person," "limited omniscient," and the other pertinent terms mean. The instructor may photocopy a list of definitions or use the glossary at the back of the book. Obviously, this exercise will work better after the class has had a basic discussion on point of view.

The instructor may collect the lists after 15 or 20 minutes, or may want to get the group together to ensure that all pairs have come up with the same answers. The instructor may also visit the various pairs and ask about one or two short stories, just to make sure certain pairs are on the right track.

Purpose: This exercise is an especially good way to review definitions without the instructor dragging the class through the glossary or eliciting responses Socratically. The burden of investigation and definition is on the students, though the instructor has several means of ensuring that the students are clear about the definitions.

3. Choose several "actors" in the class and have them do a reading of a very short story (such as Hemingway's "A Clean, Well-Lighted Place"). One actor will be The Narrator, and will read dialogue tags (he said, she said) as well as the narration.

Purpose: This exercise offers a basic way of dramatizing a story, of showing the importance of dialogue, and of having the class experience a short story as a group. Following the read-through, the instructor can lead a discussion about the effectiveness of dialogue, or about how close the story is to being a play.

4. Divide the class into groups of three to five students. Have the groups create a single thesis statement about a short story and a list of evidence to support the thesis. The instructor may have to review the definition of a thesis and how it differs from a statement of fact or a statement of summary. The instructor may also have to give some options for "evidence." A recorder in the group should write down the thesis and list the evidence.

The instructor may wander from group to group to keep the students on their task, clarify definitions, and make sure the thesis statement is just that.

After 20 or 30 minutes, recovene the class and have the recorders read the theses and the evidence. Ask the class as a whole to assess the theses and point out strengths and weaknesses.

Purpose: This exercise is a good one to try before the first paper is assigned. It gives students practice at formulating opinions, revising thesis sentences, and looking for evidence in the story. In a sense, it also introduces them to one form of the writing process.

If you are concerned that some passive or lazy students might just "lift" the group thesis for their own in their upcoming paper, you can address that issue straightforwardly; or, for the exercise, you can use a story that the students will not eventually write about.

5. To start a class session, have students read the opening paragraph or scene of a story that has been assigned. Perhaps have one student read the section out loud. Then have students close their books and quickly write down all of the imagery they remember from the paragraph or scene. Next, have the students circle three of the images they recalled and write about their significance to the story. Stress that the writing is informal and that it's intended mainly to collect their thoughts. Finish the exercise by having a few students discuss the images about which they wrote.

Purpose: This exercise is a good warm-up for a more detailed discussion of a short story. It also ensures that students have something to say, because they have jotted down what they remember and why they think the images are important. Also, the exercise is a good reinforcement of discussions about imagery and/or about showing versus telling.

6. Divide the class into groups of three to five students and tell them that the exercise will be based on three stories that they have read for that day. Tell them to assume that their group is an editorial board for an anthology of short fiction that will be locked in a vault and not published for fifty years. Tell them that all but one of the stories has been selected and that they have to select the final story from these three. Tell them to develop a few basic criteria for selection, make a selection, and then be able to justify it.

Reconvene the class as a whole and get reports from each group. It's useful for the instructor to play devil's advocate, challenging the selections in a playful way, sharpening the groups' thinking about their criteria.

Purpose: This exercise puts the students in the role of editors and forces them to articulate preferences. It also raises the issue of permanence and makes students think about why certain stories persist, what biases allow stories to persist (or disappear), and what choices go into "anthology making." It's often useful to mix a "classic" story with two fairly recent ones.

7. Have each student write a brief (one paragraph) description of a friend. The description should focus on general qualities or traits (friendliness, dependability, vanity, etc.). This should take about 10-15 minutes. The description needs to be legible. The name of the friend can be changed. Have them pass the description to the student on their right. Now have the students write a brief scene that dramatizes the general qualities in the description that they've just received. Forbid the students to repeat key words like "friendly" or "vain" or "sexy." Instead, they have to depict these qualities indirectly in the scene. The scene should be very brief and take 10-15 minutes to write.

Now have the students fold up the original description (so it can't be read) and pass it to the right with the scene that they've just written.

After they've read their colleague's scene, have them write down adjectives that describe the general qualities that they can extrapolate from the scene. That is, based on this scene, what general qualities will they ascribe to the person?

Now have the students unfold the other paper. Have them mill about, checking to see how accurate their scene conveyed the general qualities, checking to see how well they guessed the general qualities, and (of course) seeing what has happened to their friend. This process will be a bit chaotic, but the students will need to let off steam at this point anyway. At the end of the exercise, or at the beginning of the next period, use the exercise to discuss general vs. concrete descriptions and the ideas of "showing vs. telling."

This exercise will work well for both literature and creative-writing classes.

8. As a variation on Exercise Four, have the groups develop a thesis (with evidence) based on a certain "school" of criticism: New Criticism, Deconstructionism, Feminism, and so forth. Obviously, this exercise will work only in classes where different kinds of criticism have been discussed, but even if students have only an elementary understanding of different theories, the exercise can illuminate how all readers come to a text from a certain perspective. It can also allow them to "play" with certain critical perspectives.

9. Have the students write a brief monologue from the point of view of a secondary character in a story. (A story with several secondary characters will work well.) The monologues should give the characters' perspectives on the fate of the (original) main character. Have several students read these out loud and then discuss how the monologues are in themselves interpretations of the story.

Purpose: This exercise helps define what a monologue is; it dramatizes the importance of point of view (a change in point of view is a change of story); and it can get students started on an interpretation of a story. The exercise also helps students think about relationships between characters in certain stories and how these relationships create conflict. (This is a variation on the Guidelines for Interpreting Short Stories in a Group discussed earlier.)

10. Divide the class into pairs and have the pairs collaborate on a brief analysis of *one* element of a story. You may wish to assign pairs different elements from a list you have prepared. The elements can be symbols, setting, a scene, a crisis scene, the resolution, etc. Make sure at least one person in the pair writes down the interpretation. After 10-15 minutes, reconvene the class and ask for reports. After each report, ask the whole class to respond to and elaborate on the pair's interpretation.

Purpose: This exercise is a quick way to build a foundation for a group discussion of a short story. It also allows students to work out an interpretation in a process, first in the pair, then in the whole class. This process allows an interpretation to evolve and lets students see the importance of revising initial interpretations.

11. Assign pairs of students terms from the glossary and have them make brief (three to five minutes) reports on the terms. The task should be to give a more elaborate definition of a term and then find a story that exemplifies the term. The purpose here is to make students responsible not just for the definitions but for applying them. Having two students work on definitions allows them to work out problems before the oral report, and it makes the oral report less terrifying.

12. Have groups or pairs collaborate on questions for midterm or final examinations. This process allows the students to review the course and do some studying and analysis even before they take the exams. It also brings them into the process of creating examinations and allows students and teachers to talk more openly about the purpose of examinations.

Part One: Early Voices

Edgar Allan Poe, "The Tell Tale Heart"

1. His motivation might be called sociopathic because it is not connected with robbery or passion. It springs from a cold obsession with murder itself.

2. We seem to get all the facts of the murder. What the narrator cannot report accurately is what the old man really feels and also why he (the narrator) ultimately confesses. Also, he thinks he is not mad; we know he is.

3. Poe is a master of "effects," but many readers may wonder if there is anything more than shocking effects in such a story. One might make a case for his exploration of pathological states of mind and of the nature of guilt. One might also make a case for the story's being a technical experiment in unreliable narration.

4. Most readers would probably agree that the narrator's conscience, heretofore buried, finally emerges to "indict" him. The "tell-tale heart" is thus a manifestation of guilt.

Nathaniel Hawthorne, "Young Goodman Brown"

1. Hawthorne certainly teases us with this question. The narrator seems to want us to struggle with the ambiguity, and the question offers one opportunity to raise the issue of *intentional* ambiguity vs. confusion springing from shoddy story-telling.

2. If the assumption is true, we are given a man *obsessed* with good and evil, and irrationally convinced that all of Salem is wicked.

3. If the assumption is true, we are given a community that really has done the things the Devil claims. This is a good opportunity to raise a third possibility: that the community is wicked and hypocritical, and that Goodman Brown is nevertheless quite mad.

4. For Goodman Brown –and many actual early Americans –"Indians" and the wilderness represented potential evil and an unChristian wildness that needed "taming." Here is an opportunity to widen the discussion to Puritanism in general and the "errand into the wilderness."

5. There are elements of allegory here: Goodman Brown is a kind of Everyman; Faith and the woods are symbolic entitites; Goodman Brown's journey is spiritual in nature. However, Hawthorne's playfulness and purposeful ambiguity prevent us from giving the story an uncritically allegorical reading; we have to be careful.

Herman Melville, "Bartleby the Scrivener"

1. In a variety of ways the paragraph makes Bartleby extraordinary, even singular, thereby piquing our interest.

2. One purpose may be to establish a contrast between Bartleby and the other clerks. Another may be simply to give us comic portraits.

3. He is a self-described, cautious, prudent man who seems to play everything "by the book." He is a conformist for whom Bartleby's behavior is incomprehensible.

4. This question will help open up the discussion of passive resistance in general. Instructors may want to mention the philosophy of nonviolent protest important to Thoreau, Ghandi, and Martin Luther King, Jr.

5. His first response to "I prefer not to" is anger; ultimately, he develops a deep sympathy for Bartleby even if he does not understand him.

Guy de Maupassant, "The Necklace"

1. This question asks for the students' opinions. One way to pursue the question further (or differently) is to ask how much of the incident can be blamed on Mathilde's character and how much can be blamed on fate.

2. This, too, asks for the students' opinions, but it also tries to put the students in Mathilde's position.

3. This question places question 2 in wider context of social pressures and class conflict. The story is not, after all, only about one person losing a necklace but also concerns social climbing and social barriers in general.

4. This focuses on a specific technique of closure. After de Maupassant drops "the bomb" of the brutal irony, he leaves us to imagine Mathilde's reaction.

Ivan Turgenev, "Bezhin Meadow"

1. This question will help students focus on the way the two writers choose to begin their stories, and it raises the question of how description may create "mood" or "atmosphere." One tactic is to have students reread the opening paragraphs of the stories and then quickly list adjectives that describe the atmosphere the images create; then compare and contrast the adjectives to see whether patterns emerge.

2. This question will help students think about the use of the "I" narrator.

3. The tales involve (in varying degrees) the supernatural, folk wisdom, a sense of the morbid, and superstitious (perhaps!) explanations of natural phenomena.

4. Many readers may see a supernatural, "magical" quality to the narrator's descriptions.

5. The ending can be read as intentionally ambiguous. Pavel's death fits the pattern of the other calamities described, but the narrator also takes pains to explain that Pavel did *not* drown. The ending is in keeping with the narrator's complex response to the boys and their tales.

Leo Tolstoy, "The Death of Ivan Ilych"

1. Ivanovich is with the co-workers of Ilych who react in self-centered even callous ways to the news of Ivan's death. Tolstoy seems to depict Ivanovich's response in a more ambiguous, complicated way. His meeting with the widow is sometimes comic, sometimes petty, sometimes poignant.

2. Tolstoy's "roving" omniscient narrator is sometimes quite distant from Ivan and even "abandons" him for other points of view. As the story progresses, the distance may to many readers seem to shorten, and the last few pages may seem in many ways sympathetic to Ivan. Some sections focus on others' responses to Ivan's dying; others focus on his life, on his response to his own dying, and to his response to others' responses.

3. In many ways, Ivan is "the man in the gray flannel suit" an ordinary professional with ordinary problems. At times his "ordinariness" approaches smallness, pettiness. At other times it is more sympathetic. By focusing on such a character, Tolstoy may well be implying, "Here is how—more or less—all of us die, and how friends and relatives respond to deaths."

4. Ivan's response to his emotional crisis is—on the surface at least —"economic": he goes after a better-paying job.

5. He is by turns angry, resentful, and empathic. Toward the end of his life he worries more about them than he does about himself.

Anton Chekov, "Gooseberries"

1. Ivan's negative reaction to the change in his brother takes up most of the story and raises several issues, including those of "happiness" and "property." Students sometimes react to what they call "depressing" stories the way Burkin and Alyohin react to Ivan, however, so the question of how sympathetic Ivan is may be worth addressing right away.

2. The homeless, the poor, the disadvantaged—to what extent are they the "silent" bearers of burdens in our own society? This question is but one way to try to show that issues Chekhov raises are current.

3. This question will help point out the way "Gooseberries" is "layered." The story of Ivan's brother is a story within a story; Burkin and Alyohin are an unsympathetic audience to the story within a story.

4. Chekhov lets Ivan "preach" in the story, but he ends the story with imagery rather than with statement from a character, and it is worth pursuing students' interpretations of these images.

Henry James, "The Pupil"

1. We learn about Pemberton's worries concerning money; the eccentricity of Mrs Moreen; the precocity of Morgan; the naivete of Pemberton, who cannot know what Morgan will ultimately mean to him. We also learn that James believes there are numerous levels of communication and meaning in a fairly ordinary business meeting.

2. They seem to be improvident Americans abroad, with inconsistent behavior and curious relationships with their children. Morgan seems astute about his own family, particularly on the issue of economics.

3. It is extremely complicated—based in part on economics, mutual attraction, mutual "outsider" status with the family, and a certain ironic distance from events.

4. This is (as James seems to intend it) an impossible question to answer, so intertwined are the motives of the Moreens, Morgan, and Pemberton. Morgan's death is a matter of fate and predestination, but it is also a matter of all the characters in the story colliding.

Kate Chopin, "Story of an Hour"

1. Her response is ambivalent; she is grief-stricken and exhilarated. Most of all she feels liberated.

2. This paragraph is crucial to one's understanding of the ending, and to one's understanding of Louise's sense of being liberated. The question of an imposed will is one that applies directly to issues of feminism, of course, but it is also one that students may wish to explore in other contexts.

3. Paragraph 14 seems to insist that we see Louise's death springing from a realization that she will return to the prison of her husband's "will." The narrator suggests that Louise's friends will misinterpret her death and that "joy" is hardly what Louise feels.

Charlotte Perkins Gilman, "The Yellow Wallpaper"

1. Most of all she gains the sense of the woman's *voice* as the woman slowly disintegrates, victimized by her confinement and her husband's "love."

2. He seems patronizing and insensitive. He treats her like a child, and the writing seems to be one thing he can't *control*.

3. The stark paragraphing and the increasingly disoriented interpretation of events help create this sense of oncoming madness. Her perception of the wallpaper is, of course, a key element.

4. It represents her confinement, and it represents the projection of her *dementia*. It functions similarly to the pounding heart in Poe's story in that it *focuses* her madness.

Arthur Conan Doyle, "A Scandal in Bohemia"

1. Many critics and casual readers have observed that Watson is just as interesting as Holmes is as a character—and that he is a complicated narrator. "A Scandal in Bohemia" is a story that illuminates Watson well, but it is also one of the rare stories that shows Watson in a slightly superior position to Holmes.

2. This story is a good one for getting a sense of Holmes' personality and methods. He is very much the cold, dispassionate reasoner here; in fact, one purpose of the story seems to be that Irene Adler was able to pierce that armor. The story also shows us Holmes as the detective who loves disguises, and it's a good idea to explore with students the attraction disguises might have for a person like Holmes. A good follow-up question to this one: "Is Watson correct in characterizing Holmes' mind as "balanced'? Why or why not?" One might also mention the "Freudian" version of Holmes we get in *The Seven Per Cent Solution*.

3. There are several detective "types" with which students may want to contrast Holmes: hard-boiled (Raymond Chandler's Marlowe, Dashiell Hammett's Spade, etc.); soft-boiled (Spenser, Magnum); women detectives (from Agatha Christie's sleuths to Sarah Peretsky's); police (starting with those that appear in the Holmes stories themselves); spies; and so on.

4. It's interesting (predictable?) that Holmes, the unconventional, super-rational detective, is also a conventional, irrational thinker when it comes to women. Irene Adler is an unusual character for Doyle because she is not a victim. One issue that is worth exploring with students is the extent to which Irene Adler is a prototype for the femme fatale that shows up in so many detective stories later. It's also worth asking the extent to which Watson's view of Adler differs from Holmes' view.

5. The purpose of this question is to get students to think about the detective story as a subgenre, and to engage them in some inductive literary criticism, whereby they generate the "rules" of a subgenre by looking at just one story. "A Scandal in Bohemia" has the following ingredients (among others): a crime, a victim, an amateur detective who sometimes gets paid but whose motive for working is not money, a dangerous woman, a sidekick, a "sting" operation that fails, an exotic element (the King of Bohemia).

O. Henry, "The Gift of the Magi"

1. The narrator seems quite distant from Della and her predicament. The tone may be sardonic.

2. In a sense, O. Henry includes a "moral" at the end of his tale. This question offers one way to discuss the concept of "showing vs. telling."

3. Conventional wisdom says that plot is everything in O. Henry stories, but students may not agree. Another way to ask the question is to ask which story—O. Henry's or Chekhov's (for instance)—is more like a television show.

4. This asks for the students' opinions and gets at the question of how *they* define an excellent story.

Sholem Aleichem, "On Account of a Hat"

1. An "I" narrator narrates; Kasrilkevke tells the story; Sholem Shachnah is the main character.

2. He is hapless, a "rattlebrain" who often gets outwitted and who often outwits himself. He is like the comic figure that appears in many Yiddish tales.

3. Since we know that Shachnah can be officious, the fact that he dons an official hat is appropriate.

4. He is garrulous and insistent, self-conscious and ironic. His asides flavor the physical comedy with added wit.

Stephen Crane, "The Blue Hotel"

1. From the first moment he is portrayed as odd—nervous, guilty, out-of-place, unfriendly.

2. He indicates immediately that he is afraid of being killed, and then goes on to act obnoxiously in a place where being obnoxious results in violence.

3. This statement seems to suggest that blind forces, not unlike the storm, define the fate of humans and that to pretend otherwise is an example of conceit.

4. Toward the end of the story, the narrator suggests that, except for being obnoxious, the Swede is actually more "upright" morally than other citizens.

5. The end of the story makes it plain that the man did cheat and that, in one sense, the Swede was in the right. It reinforces the sense that the Swede's death was a product of rage and other blind forces and in no sense a product of "justice," poetic or otherwise.

Joseph Conrad, "The Secret Sharer"

1. Both the crew and the captain are waiting to see what kind of captain he will be and whether he will seize authority. Therefore, seemingly unimportant nuances of behavior become crucial. Also, the captain seems to link the issue of authority with an "ideal of personality" he has established for himself.

2. Conrad seems to create plenty of "clues" for both interpretations, making this story a rich source of discussion about ideals of personality, personality and positions of authority, split personalities and "the divided self," unreliable narration, and so forth. It may be useful to mention other stories of "the double" in the nineteenth century: Poe's "William Wilson," Stevenson's "Dr. Jekyll and Mr. Hyde," Twain's "The Prince and the Pauper," James Hogg's *Confessions of a Justified Sinner*.

3. In addition to questions of personality and reliable narration, the story also concerns ethical behavior and "the law of the sea."

4. This question specifically addresses the issue (and technique) of "unreliable narration." It is worth pointing out that stories which turn out to be "all a dream" or otherwise totally unreliable often make readers feel cheated, and that Conrad works with a more ambiguous form of unreliability.

Part Two: Modern Voices

James Joyce, "Araby"

1. He is infatuated with her. He idealizes her and, in his mind, associates her with romantic imagery.

2. He functions as a foil for the boy's romantic notions. He is uncooperative, unsympathetic, vulgar—part of the world that the boy finally confronts at the end of the story.

3. At the end of the story, the boy confronts something in himself and in "being human" that he has not confronted before: vanity and hopelessness. The ambience of the bazaar and his failure to buy something seem to trigger this moment of "sight" or "revelation" or "epiphany."

4. The illusions of idealized love and romance are taken from him. In a sense, the whole day's events have conspired with his innocence to drive him to this moment of new consciousness.

D. H. Lawrence, "The Horse Dealer's Daughter"

1. The family is presented as one that is spiritually as well as financially degraded, and the image of the great draught-horses swinging past is a key Lawrentian image of freedom, power, even sexuality. Mabel is presented in this early part of the story as a woman horribly dominated by her stupid, callous brothers—a woman who has been emotionally caged.

2. The point of view seems to be omniscient, moving in and out of various minds, giving us the thoughts of one of the brothers, of Mabel, and of Jack.

3. Many readers will see that the pond evokes a sense both of Eros and Thanatos—sexuality and death. In a sense, Jack and Mabel are "reborn"—however briefly—when they emerge from the muck in which Mabel has tried to kill herself. Later, Lawrence seems to suggest that their reborn passion and sexuality quickly falls prey to conventions, to guilt, to shame, and to language (or "speaking love").

Ernest Hemingway, "A Clean, Well-Lighted Place"

1. This dialogue begins to reveal the differences between the waiters and their perception of the old man. One is sympathetic, or at least neutral, while the other one can muster no sympathy.

2. In his despair and lack of faith, the older waiter seems to place great emphasis on "venues" that are at least tolerable, and he seems to value a kind of orderliness and professionalism. One way to interpret his point of view is to say that he tries to live in "the here and now"; another might be to say that he is "shoring fragments against his ruin," to borrow from Eliot. In any event, there seems to be a philosophical purpose, and not just a whim, behind his infatuation with "a clean, well-lighted place."

3. One understands what the old man is going through and empathizes with his reasons for attempting suicide. The other apparently hasn't confronted such basic existential questions and views the old man and his problems as a bother.

4. It is not so much sacrilegious as it is a poignant parody (if such a thing is possible), a matter-of-fact statement of faithlessness and despair. It is still very much a prayer, oddly enough—a kind of meditation on hopelessness, certainly not an attack on religion.

Franz Kafka, "A Hunger Artist"

1. This asks the students to speculate. Some possibilities are rock bands that rely on images and lyrics of violence, or daredevils that make an "art" out of coming close to death. Of course, to imply that the hunger artist (or these other artists) is perverse is to beg the question, so one might also ask the class to define and argue about the limits of perversity during the discussion.

2. The where and the when of the story are unclear, giving the story an eerie, unfixed quality and enhancing its parable-like nature. One might compare and contrast it with fairy tales in this regard, because fairy tales often take place in "the forest," for example.

3. There is a matter-of-fact, deadpan quality to the narration, as if hunger artists were everywhere and as if the events related were not out of the ordinary.

4. One is always tempted to ask such questions of Kafka's writing, but such questions are frustrating because Kafka rarely if ever "gives anything away," pointing us to easy symbolic interpretations. The fact that the hunger artist makes an art out of a basic appetite, the fact that he is exploited, the fact that the crowd is morbidly attracted to him—these and other elements of the story suggest, at least, that Kafka has found a way to look into the complicated nature of human desires and human "performance."

William Faulkner "A Rose for Emily"

1. "The town"—or "we"—narrates the story, so although the story is in first person, the narrative voice is oddly general and vague, and actions are ascribed to "one of us" or "several citizens." This narrative technique is strikingly appropriate because it enhances the sense we have of Emily's eccentricity and isolations—the ways in which she is not a part of the town and the "we."

2. This task will enable the students to see how richly figurative Faulkner's style is. (In class one might quickly turn to Hemingway's story and read part of it to see how relatively unfigurative his style is.) It will also build a foundation for discussing Emily as a symbolic character, for even the first description of her suggests that she is "submerged" and even dead.

3. Garages and new homes have "encroached and obliterated" the old neighborhood. Emily's fall from pseudo-aristocracy has been paralleled by the "fall" of the neighborhood. The images are of conflict, even warfare, echoing the 1860s.

4. Homer Baron is a Yankee and a working-class person. He is handsome and attractive, but he also represents forces in the South that have eroded Miss Emily's heritage and the assumptions by which she has always lived.

5. Miss Emily represents the past. She represents a certain kind of young Southern woman grown old, and she represents old-fashioned assumptions about womanhood, courtship, and "society."

Frank O'Connor, "Guests of the Nation"

1. They get along very well. They play cards, and the Englishmen help the old woman. Curiously, when they argue, they argue not about the issues of the civil war, but about communism and capitalism, and about the causes of another war (WWI). They do not behave as enemies.

2. Belcher is quieter and somewhat less opinionated. Hawkins tries to bargain for his life and says that, because he believes in nothing, he would just as soon join the Irish side. Belcher becomes talkative before his death, wanting to pour out his life story, but not wanting to bargain: he seems resigned. Courageously, he asks that they shoot Hawkins once more so that Hawkins' suffering can be ended.

3. He says that those who talk about duty never see troubled by duty, hinting that "duty" may be a term for what people want to do, not what they have to do. After the Holocaust and the Nuremberg trials, the word "duty" reverberates even more.

4. Because of the references to World War I, some students may be confused about which war is the background to this story. It is the Irish/English civil war; the narrator is a member of the Irish Republican Army.

5. The old woman acts as a kind of conscience and as a modified form of a Greek Chorus. Her comment about "disturbing the hidden powers," which comes at the end of section one, is obviously ominous. Her reaction to the news of the Englishmen's execution is in stark contrast to the narrator's. He is driven to a kind of faithlessness. She is thrown back on her faith.

Luigi Pirandello, "War"

1. This asks for the students' opinions. Many of the students may actually be interested in the particulars of the debate; others may sense that the debate is awfully cerebral and artificial—a point that the ending of the story drives home.

2. The woman is compared to a bundle, and Pirandello crafts some remarkable images depicting the faces of these older Italians, particularly the face of the man who breaks down at the end of the story.

3. It is ironic that the woman's simple, direct question cuts through the issues of the debate and deflates the overblown, artificial nature of the debate. Her question makes all of the fine distinctions pointless, and it devastates the man who had argued so coolly.

4. It is at least interesting to point out that the men talk a great deal and frame the question in fairly abstract terms while the woman asks a concrete questions that somehow gets to the heart of the matter.

Tadeusz Borowski, "The Supper"

1. The portrait of the soldiers shows not just brutality but madness; it also recalls Hannah Arendt's now-famous comment about the banality of evil.

2. Most readers will perceive a certain detachment in the attitude of the narrator, a matter-of-factness that lets the brutality and evil speak for itself.

3. The last scene shifts our attention from the brutality of the soldiers to the effect of that brutality on prisoners. The prisoners have been stripped of human dignity.

4. Such a story raises numerous questions about the relationship between writing and the Holocaust. George Steiner, among others, has said that in some ways silence is the only rational response to such utterly irrational evil. But others, including Elie Wiesel, say that to record the evil—to keep the memory of it alive—is absolutely necessary. Borowski's story speaks the unspeakable; its images are impossible to forget. Inevitably there are students who want literature to be not only uplifting but also pretty, and such students will resist not just the story but the questions it raises.

Aya Koda, "The Black Kimono"

1. The story begins several years before the end of World War II and ends about the time of the destruction of Hiroshima, which is mentioned toward the end of the story.

2. It is a very complicated relationship, to say the least. Ko seems to want to maintain a certain authority over her. Also, the social customs seem to demand reticence. Nonetheless, there is also evidence of great afffection between them. The fact that they always meet at funerals makes their relationship poignant—and odd.

3. She becomes increasingly detached and cynical. It might be a good idea to contrast her emotions at the start of the story with her emotions during the last funeral.

4. The war is certainly in the background, but to some extent this is a story about a woman whose life is almost dedicated to "serving" death and destruction, so in this sense it is a war story.

Sherwood Anderson, "The Egg"

1. This question is, of course, impossible to answer, but it is a question the narrator himself seem concerned about. There is a sense in which the fates conspire against everything the father tries, but "the triumph of the egg" also suggests that there is something in the father's small-town Ohio characters that drives him to want things he should not want, and to try things that he is not equipped to succeed at. The question is useful for students who have confronted the "nature vs. nurture" issue in other courses, and it is useful for students writing their own stories and working out the question of "fate vs. character" in fictional terms.

2. The tone of narration is oddly detached and ironic, as if the son were writing from a substantial temporal, spatial, and emotional "distance." To some extent he speaks of his father with wry sadness, and to some extent he examines his father's fate almost clinically.

3. This question asks for the students' opinions, but it also offers an opportunity to *begin* to define "comic" and "tragic," those hopelessly large terms. One might bring up the terms "vanity" and "hubris" and talk about the ways in which the father is full of "pride." One might also ask the students the extent to which the father's fate is "our" fate —the extent to which we sympathize with his misguided desires, that is.

4. "The egg" seems to be a symbol for the whole question of "character vs. fate," particularly with its echoes of genetics, on the one hand, and "chicken vs. egg" on the other.

Katherine Anne Porter, "The Jilting of Granny Weatherall"

1. It shows her to be tough, brittle, and outspoken. It also begins to suggest how alone she is.

2. One can "deconstruct" "Weatherall" in a number of ways, but it seems to reflect her tenacity and to suggest the ways in which she has been battered by life.

3. Granny seems to connect the two in this way: She has done her part. She was faithful to him—and to Him—and she has been jilted by both. She has been reduced to her iron will, to her ferocious intent to hold up her end of the bargain, even as life slips away.

4. She becomes increasingly confused, mixing past with present and hallucination with perception, even as she becomes more focused on her connection with God and the jilting that occurred in the past.

John Steinbeck, "The Chrysanthemums"

1. We find out how assertive Elisa is in their relationship, how reserved and somewhat backward Henry is, and how capable Elisa is, not just with gardening but in general. Their personalities are clearly established.

2. She is an intelligent person who nonetheless seems lonely and in need of praise. To some extent her husband seems unaware of the things she's interested in and of her desires. The tinker seems to sense these needs, and he exploits them.

3. Probably she doesn't tell Henry because she is embarrassed, but also because she probably can't share her emotional life with him. What made her vulnerable to the tinker is what prevents her from telling her husband about how vulnerable she was.

4. The setting contributes to the sense we have both of Elisa's "earthiness" and of the circumstances of her isolation.

Eudora Welty, "Petrified Man"

1. Welty keeps misspellings to a minimum. In one sentence, for example, she misspells only "yestiddy." By misspelling one word Welty gives us the flavor, or effect, of the dialect without attempting to "record" the conversation with dozens of misspelled words. She also captures the rhythm of conversation—and the way Leota and Mrs. Fletcher "miscommunicate" by not listening, changing the subject whimsically, being self-absorbed, etc.

2. Their attitudes change because Mrs. Pike's fortune changes; Mrs. Pike escapes, and they cannot.

3. Billy Boy's question is an indictment of the two women, and it is a repetition of the pettiness and meanness that they have exhibited throughout the story.

Willa Cather, "Paul's Case"

1. The descriptions reveal his unstable, seemingly doomed character.

2. He is erratic and desperate; his motives are confused. In connection with this question, one might explore the extent to which the students sympathize with Paul's behavior and choices.

3. The narrator seems detached, removed, perhaps even clinical. One might have students first list adjectives to describe either the narrator or "the tone" of the story.

4. For many readers, it may function as a symbol of Paul's demise.

Ralph Ellison, "King of the Bingo Game"

1. The opening of the story gives us marvelous details about how desperately hungry and thirsty the man is, how exhausted he is, and how deperate he is to take care of his family. He is also shown to be very much a foreigner in this big northern city.

2. The man is convinced that he can control the wheel, win the game, and escape his terrible circumstances. It gives him an illusory sense of control and power and becomes a token of his insanity.

3. To be king of a bingo game is in itself an odd kind of royalty. Worse, the man is in fact not king of (in control of) the bingo wheel; it controls him, just as social circumstances have controlled him.

Langston Hughes, "On the Road"

1. It is possible to take the snow to represent the white world against which Sargeant has to struggle. (He is more aware of the snow when he becomes more aware of the church's refusal to help him, for example.) The "doors of opportunity" (shelter, food) are closed to Sargeant because he is black; the doors of the jail hold him in for the same reason. Only the hoboes' jungles are without doors, ironically.

2. It is interesting that the Christ in Sargeant's dream is glad to be freed from the cross, as if organized religion has kept Him on the cross as a way of refusing to be genuinely Christian. It is poignant, too, to see how much of Sargeant's personality gets into the Christ of his dream. Like Sargeant, Christ is hungry, homeless, and abandoned.

3. This question asks for the students' opinions, but homelessness is such a widely discussed issue that students are bound to see some relevance in Hughes' story.

Zorah Neale Hurston, "Sweat"

1. Many elements of the conflict are present in this scene: Sykes' violence, Delia's rebellion, and clearly a sense that this is an abusive relationship, a struggle for power.

2. Sykes is violent and abusive. He also underestimates Delia.

3. One way to interpret the snake is as a symbol of Sykes' violence, which "comes back to haunt him," in a sense. The snake is also a device that enables us to see Delia surviving by her wits, by "negotiating" her way around her violent, abusive husband. The snake also seems to be a recapitulation of the bullwhip in the first scene.

4. It is a complicated response, full of relief and horror and awe.

Raymond Chandler, "The Wrong Pigeon"

1. He is the prototype for the hard-boiled detective: cool under pressure; tough on the outside but often sentimental on the inside; a person of considerable scruples (he resists taking the money, for instance); a person who seems to relish violence and who is an outsider, a kind of "knight errant" caught between official police and the criminal world. Marlowe shares this last characteristic with Holmes, but in other ways he is more brutal and less purely cerebral than Holmes. He also tends to work on grubbier cases than Holmes does.

2. It is a terse, "flat" style, though it tends to include more metaphors and similes than Hemingway's brand of the hard-boiled style. It also depends heavily on the diffident first-person "voice" of the detective, so in this sense it differs from a journalistic, reportorial style.

3. This is an impossible "either/or" question, of course, but it is intended to help students explore one paradox of detective fiction: while we think of it as action-oriented and dependent on intricate plotting, the real attraction of the genre (beginning with Conan Doyle and Poe) is often the personality of the protagonist. We tend to forget plots and to remember detectives.

4. The motivation of hard-boiled detectives is legendarily ambiguous. Sometimes he seems "purely" motivated, wanting to do good in a bad world; at other times he is out for revenge; at other times he seems to relish immersing himself in a dangerous, violent life; and at other times he needs the money.

Katherine Mansfield, "The Fly"

1. We cannot know Mansfield's intentions or purpose, of course, but one effect of the shift seems to be to start in the consciousness of someone who is disabled and trapped, rather like the fly. Also, the older man himself forgets what he wants to tell "the boss," so that a pattern of fickleness begins, establishing a context for what Mansfield wants to portray about the fleeting nature of human grief and emotions.

2. This asks for the students' opinions, but many of us may grudgingly have to admit that the boss's treatment of the fly is rather typical.

3. Mansfield casts a rather cold eye toward grief in this story. In the story, emotions come and go in a haphazard, unpredictable way; the man forgets his sorrow almost instantaneously.

Yasunari Kawabata, "The Mole"

1. The mole comes to represent a great many things: the speaker's "secret world" or private view of herself; a source of rebellion against her husband; a token of their abusive relationship; sexuality; identity; a token of her childhood; and a symbol of the so-called "bad wife."

2. The narrator speaks directly to the husband. One effect may be to make readers feel as if they are "listening in" on a private conversation. Another effect may be to dramatize the oppressive nature of their relationship, for the narrator is clearly obsessed with the husband's power and what the husband thinks of the mole.

3. From the first moment, we sense that he has tremendous power over her and that she feels oppressed by him. She also seems to discover that he does not love her. Later in the story we discover that their relationship is not just psychologically abusive but also physically abusive.

Part Three: Contemporary Voices

John Updike, "A & P"

1. He's an honest, colloquial, observant speaker, full of energy, opinions, and a bit of bitterness. The narration makes him seem like a rapid speaker and a believable, young, working-class character.

2. The fact that a bathing suit scandalizes the customers and Lengel suggests something about the town, the neighborhood, and perhaps the times themselves. Also, Sammy himself (by means of the images of the different ways in which his and Queenie's families socialize) raises the issue of a conflict between middle-class "beach" families and working-class "town" families. There also seems to be a conflict suggested between duty and family (on the one hand) and sexuality, passion, protest (on the other). Lengel and Stokesie are conventional. Queenie—at least in this situation—is not. Sammy is forced to choose.

3. This asks for the students' opinions, but it may be worth guiding the students to consider whether Sammy himself thinks this is an effective protest (he seems to know that it's futile). Also, it will be interesting to ask students what they would do in a similar situation.

4. Stokesie represents the near-future of marriage and a young family. Lengel represents the more distant future of being a boring, stuffy, prudish manager.

5. This asks the students to perform a task; it is designed to emphasize a strength in Updike's writing that critics have praised from the beginning: his eye for sharp, telling details.

John Cheever, "Goodbye, My Brother"

1. This asks for the students' opinions, but you may want to draw out specific examples of how their families believe in this illusion. You may also want to explore why families believe in their uniqueness.

2. The image foreshadows the violence at the end of the story.

3. This asks for the students' opinions, but one might argue that "circumspection" involves a kind of timidity and retreat, whereas character involves not just restraint but commitment and affirmation, qualities Lawrence does not have.

4. This asks for the students' views of the narrator and his attack on Lawrence. One possibility is to ask how they would have handled a difficult sibling like Lawrence, or to ask what alternatives to violence the narrator had.

5. Lawrence sees the worst in everything, from buildings to people. He resists socializing and sees dark motives in games and parties. He cuts himself off from people at any sign of weakness, excess, or imperfection. He oppresses his wife, Ruth.

Janet Frame, "Insulation"

1. It is a playful allusion, especially in the way it conflates two scenes, personifies nature (or "the country"), and changes the famous quotation. On the serious side it is a reference to nature being poised at a turning point, just as Hamlet is during his famous speech. The countryside is about to "turn," and the people of Stratford instinctively "prepare" (though of course one point of the story is that one cannot prepare in some respects).

2. Specifically, she connects the economic use of the term "shedding" with the shedding of leaves, but in general she depicts inevitable economic change, just as a change in seasons is inevitable. Later, economics (the man's new job) and nature link up by means of "insulation"; the man's last stab at economic well-being (his own insulation from demise) is to sell insulation.

3. It collects and transforms all of the characters that have been introduced and places them in a kind of fairy tale—one that does not turn out all right.

4. Certainly the disturbing dream seems to create guilt in her. We have seen that she is an empathic person, not above an ironic view of middle-class "buying," but also willing to see that everyone is a potential victim of arbitrary economic changes. At some level she recognizes a kinship with the man who has lost his job.

5. It seems to take on the meaning of "protection" in general—from the cold, from economic reality, from inevitable change. It seems to represent the guarantee against change that all of us seek from time to time.

Alice Munro, "Miles City, Montana"

1. The opening scene is cinematic in the particularity and drama of its detail, including the man walking across the field carrying the dead boy. That it is her father who carries the boy is significant insofar as it connects with the other fathers (and parents) of the story, including Steve's and the narrator's husband. This is very much a story of parental implication, and the opening images establish that pattern indirectly.

2. He is a rough loner of a boy, with a combination of cruelty and warmth reminiscent of Vincent Sabella in Richard Yates' story, "Doctor Jack-o'-lantern." Like many adolescent relationships, Steve's and the narrator's is love/hate in nature.

3. When I have used this story in class, some students at first complain that the car trip is "too long" and that the two parts of the story don't connect. The car trip is crucial, though, because it is full of suggestions about "character vs. fate" and "accident vs. responsibility." The narrator's thoughts, her ruminations about the girls' different personalities, the guessing game they play, the tension between wife and husband: these and other elements of the trip prepare us not just for the near-drowning but for the narrator's interpretations of that event and, in retrospect, of Steve Gauley's drowning. In structuring this story, Munro demands patience from the reader and therefore risks losing some readers. Emphasizing the cinematic quality of the story throughout may assist the discussion of the story.

5. The narrator seems to suggest that there is more arbitrariness and accident involved in deaths than we are often willing to admit, and she suggests that children have the temerity to question this arbitrariness and to be angry with adults, either for accepting "accident" too coolly or for pretending that the world is not accidental. She also suggests that her husband tries to explain away the near-death of their daughter.

Ann Beattie, "In the White Night"

1. The game is meant to be harmless, but of course it makes Carol (and Vernon) think of their daughter's death, which they are always thinking about at some level, but which they might wish to push aside on this evening.

2. He is kind but reserved, a person whose self-esteem seems to depend greatly on how much "good" he does for others. The fact that he knocks wine glasses over and follows Carol in attempts to "contain" her crying is one memorable detail of his personality.

3. They grieve in an odd way on this evening. One lies on the couch, and the other lies beside the couch. But one point of the story seems to be that few ways of grieving are inappropriate, and that each day requires "adjustments" that may strike some as quirks.

4. Some of the emotion is reported through Carol's consciousness and her assessment of things, but much of it is expressed or reinforced by sharp imagery, carefully observed gestures, and the atmosphere of "the white night," which seems to become a symbolic setting for this understated drama of grief.

Hisaye Yamamoto, "Yoneko's Earthquake"

1. Specifically, they lead to her choice not to believe in the Christian God as He has been described to her. In more general terms, they add up to "a season of disappointment," a rite of passage into a world whose brutality is more apparent to her. Many of the events are arbitrary; others are willfully cruel.

2. There is a naivete to the reporting, especially in the list of Marpo's "achievements," which are themselves naive attempts at self-improvement or self-advertisement. The naivete gives us a sense of Yoneko's innocence, provides astonishing moments of wry humor, and stands in contrast to the brutality that is reported. The tone here may remind some readers of Huckleberry Finn, though the latter is in first person, not third.

3. She decides not to believe in Him.

4. This asks for the students' opinions, but may be useful to talk about crises of faith—in any religion—and what causes them.

5. Marpo charms her with the "poem," "Don't be funny, honey!" Her father's racist remarks about Filipinos quickly fade from her mind. We don't know for sure, but presumably Mr. Hosoume asks him to leave, partly because Marpo has witnessed the physical abuse of his wife. To some extent, Marpo represents "the outside world," the world Yoneko's father cannot rule or contain. He entertains and charms Yoneko and even begins to be a love interest of sorts by giving her the inexpensive ring, which she fears her parents will notice and which they don't, partly because they are so preoccupied.

Richard Yates, "Doctor Jack-o'-lantern"

1. This asks for the students' opinions, but chances are they will see universal elements in the way Vincent is "greeted": the staring, the giggling, the shunning—and the way the teacher's best efforts backfire.

2. The story is told through the minds of Miss Price and Vincent, but their thoughts are reported by a narrator who is fairly detached and cool, especially in his assessment of Miss Price. The point of view is not omniscient because it is limited to two characters, but it is unusual insofar as it does include two characters. The point of view seems to work well because it provides us with both the motives and the actions of Miss Price and Vincent, showing us how misguided she is and how vulnerable he is.

3. This calls for speculation, but certainly one could argue that Vincent lies to try to seem important, to fit in, and to try to make up for his impoverished background.

4. He seems to want revenge and attention at the same time. He clearly wants Miss Price's approval, but he seems uncertain as to how to receive it, and he is also angry at being an outsider and (perhaps) at the failure of Miss Price to ensure his acceptance. His rage is certainly justifiable.

5. Things do not look good for Vincent, especially since the classmates have written him off as a backward person and a liar and Miss Price has already given him only one more chance. One can envision Vincent running way or committing other inappropriate "crimes" against the school.

6. In this instance, and in most instances, confusion about a name is confusion about identity. He has not been "identified" by this group or in it. Despite all of her god will, Miss Price does not listen well enough to find out what *he* wants to be called; the students use the confusion to tease him, and finally the students twist the mistake he made in class into *their* name for him. The power to identify is entirely theirs.

Cynthia Ozick, "The Butterfly and the Traffic Light"

1. This asks for the students' opinions.

2. The narrator says that streets of ancient cities have a layered, textured history and that they are important not because of name but because of function. The opposite, she says, is true of streets in American cities.

3. The history of this city reveals a certain self-importance, a painful "newness" and lack of history, and a narrow-mindedness.

4. To him they seem ephemeral and decorative.

5. Fishbein doesn't like the way she argues, nor does he like the fact that she *does* argue. He wants his lectures to be heard, not questioned.

6. What we get is a series of analogies and metaphors aimed at elaborating on the ahistorical, ephemeral, ambitious nature of small American cities.

Flannery O'Conner, "Everything That Rises Must Converge"

1. It tells and shows us how insufferable the mother is, how much Julian despises—and yet depends on—her. It also sets up the eventual confrontation because it shows how narrow-minded the mother is and how arrogant Julian is in his supposedly enlightened view.

2. She is condescending.

3. Julian is ecstatic because he thinks his mother's experience on the bus is giving her a lesson. The rest of the question asks for the students' opinions.

4. In his view they undermine the mother's sense of how different she is from people of color.

5. The woman strikes Julian's mother because Julian's mother has been unbearably intrusive, condescending, and insulting. The resolution shocks Julian and explodes his hubris. The ending is an example of dramatic irony because it is Julian who pays for the lesson that he has wanted his mother to receive, so in a sense it is he who has received the lesson. It is also dramatically ironic because the reader knows more than Julian, who thinks he knows everything.

Tim O'Brien, "The Things They Carried"

1. O'Brien creates a cumulative effect by showing what the soldiers were required to carry (which shows what a soldier's life is like), what they chose to carry (which shows us particular soldier's personalities), and what they clung to (a picture, a Bible, etc.), which in some cases shows us what they did to cope with death, danger, and fear. Eventually, then, the story gets at the heart of the experience through these lists and elaborations of their meaning.

2. O'Brien organizes the story in lists, under categories, but within the lists he fashions narratives and sketches and "drifts" from the list, per se, only to tether the story again to another list.

3. O'Brien shows us more than things; he shows us why they carried what they carried.

4. They are stunned, of course, but, perhaps in part to cope, each soldier focuses on a highly particular element of the death, such as how he fell, or the irony of what he was doing when he was shot, or (in Cross' case) where the blame should lie.

5. This asks for the students' responses.

6. He seems to suggest that language itself was a means of survival, that it provided soldiers with a medium to respond to death and fear, and that it also shaped a soldier's role or identity in Vietnam.

Margaret Atwood, "Rape Fantasies"

1. The story suggests that the "fantasies" these women have are not, in fact, about rape. The fantasies may be about seduction and erotic encounters, but one point of the story, perhaps, is that rape is an act of violence that springs from viewing the victim as an object and only an object, that it is an act of rage, and that it is the opposite of seduction and erotica. Within this context, the story also obliquely dismisses the idea that victims somehow "ask" to be raped.

2. The naive narrator is an unusual but effective choice, especially for a story that might be considered "topical" or "issue-oriented." For by choosing such a narrator, Atwood avoids preachiness. But more importantly, she creates a narrator who is simple but not simple-minded. Her simplicity and lack of pretentiousness allow her to pierce through the nonsense of her fellow workers and, with some struggle, get to the heart of rape, showing rape to be a violent act that obliterates the humanity of the victim.

3. At one point the narrator shows that she is aware that many rapes are committed not by strangers to the victim but by acquaintances, co-workers, etc. This is one more instance in which she has cut through the unreality of her co-workers' notions of rape.

4. They are not about rape but are fantasies of seduction.

5. This asks for the students' opinions.

Ray Bradbury, "2002: Night Meeting"

1. He is not a superhero or a spaceship captain but a laborer driving to work in a pickup.

2. The conflict is between different perceptions of Time and how it is manifested in the landscape or in Space. The conflict seems to spring from an Einsteinian notion of the universe, in which the shape of Time and Space depends upon where (and when) you are. One might argue that Bradbury's story is an allegory of Einsteinian physics.

3. In one key paragraph he explicitly names objects and processes and sensory qualities associated with Time, all of which are filtered through Tomas' point of view. In addition, the whole story is implicitly about different perceptions of Time's passage.

4. It is not a story that draws heavily either on mythic adventure or technology. It springs from a concern for perception and psychology.

Carlos Fuentes, "Aura"

1. This asks for the students' responses, but you may want to raise the issue of whether the "you" voice is too visible and monotonous in comparison with first and third person. You may also want to refer students to the novel *Bright Lights, Big City* (Jay McInerny), which is written entirely in the second person. Technically, the reader does become the narrator, but most readers probably still visualize "someone else" thinking the thoughts and performing the actions.

2. He is tempted by the opportunity to make money, by how well the ad fits his talents, by the mystery of the neighborhood, by the opportunity to delve into the past, by the beauty of Aura, by the fantasy of eternal youth.

3. It is significant, of course, because it suggests a spiritual presence, not a physical one. The definitions of "aura" include "an invisible emanation or vapor," "a particular atmosphere or quality that seems to surround or arise from a person or thing," and "a warning sensation that precedes a seizure of other neurological disorder" (*Webster's New World Dictionary*, Second College Edition).

4. The gothic elements are legion, including the ancient neighborhood with confusing addresses, the ancient dark house, the mysterious old woman, the musty papers, and the air of death, tragedy, and doom.

5. These disagreements give us a hint as to Aura's identity. Technically Aura does not live in the present so she does not notice what the narrator notices. The disagreements also create some dramatic irony, for the reader begins to sense trouble earlier than the supposedly intelligent narrator does (provided that, with the second person, we can separate narrator and reader). At the end of the story, the disjunctive perceptions join together as the narrator takes on Consuelo's knowledge.

6. He is just bright enough to be attracted by the scheme, to fool himself into thinking that he is in control, and to think too highly of the things he manages to figure out (such as Consuelo's age). He is classically hubristic.

7. The seductive quality of the past, the yearning for eternal youth, the conflict between cool reason and overwhelming passion, the conflict between "Eros" and "Thanatos"—these are among the themes that the story projects.

Lars Gustafsson, "Uncle Sven and the Cultural Revolution"

1. Sven thinks neither project is possible, but he is long-suffering, and he will try.

2. He is typical in that he relies on facts and figures and he is precise. His reflectiveness and flexibility might be atypical.

3. This asks for the students' opinions.

4. They are obstinate and arrogantly powerful.

5. He tries to "fit in," reading from "the little red book," but there is a practical side to him that makes him want to convince them not to pursue the propeller project.

6. It suggests a man peacefully retiring, and it suggests that his generosity toward the Chinese has been noticed.

Bernard Malamud, "The Jewbird"

1. It does feature a talking, thinking animal, but the tone and plot are comic in nature, adding a significant flavor of exuberant humor and irony.

2. This question asks for the students' opinions, but you may want to follow up by asking what the story suggests about prejudice in general or Anti-Semitism specifically.

3. Schwartz is irreverent, funny, and smart.   In German, *schwarz* means black.

4. He has developed an irrational suspicion of and hatred for the bird.

5. It is garrulous and ironic, borrowing very much from an oral tradition.   It is a tone that certainly does not take itself too seriously.

Heinrich Böll, "My Melancholy Face"

1. The fact that the narrator is absolutely minding his own business when he is arrested, the fact that he is arrested for exactly the opposite reason for which he was arrested earlier, and the behavior of the various police officials (and the older citizen) are some of the elements that convey the sense of totalitarianism.

2. He is passive, wry, and diffident, and merely reports the abuses he suffers.

3. They seemed designed to control every element of behavior in the society.

4. He decides that he must have "no face," which is a symbol for disappearing as an individual, of course.

5. The obvious answer is that Germany created its own kind of completely arbitrary, destructive, and totalitarian state under Adolph Hitler and the National Socialist Party. The less obvious answer is that the Germany of today, and of Heinrich Böll, is and was divided between capitalist democracy and communist totalitarianism.

Donald Barthelme, "The Author"

1. It's an interesting study of the "proverb" we sometimes use to describe fiction—"the lie that tells the truth"—because for all his obsession with facts, the narrator unwittingly convinces most of us that the author is fairly accurate in her portrait of her children, and that he is missing the point of her fiction. It also suggests the author is really one who invents worlds, not one who imitates them or reports them.

2. He is a bit of a nit-picker, and he is humorless, but he is also intelligent in a narrow, self-limiting way.

3. It suggests that the narrator has misinterpreted the relationship between the author (the mother) and her children, which is clearly one of power, and one in which she holds the power. From her point of view, she invents her children, just as she invents characters; indeed, Barthelme blurs the line between fact and fiction, character and "real" person, author, and parent.

Joyce Carol Oates, "The Murder"

1. In numerous ways, Oates transforms "crime" fiction. The form of the story immediately puts into doubt whether the murder has occurred or will occur. The artificial frame of fiction is self-consciously broken when the narrator says that she may now enter the story. Also, who the detective is, who the murderer is, what the motivations are—these and other classic elements are all deliberately distorted or confused, so that what we get is a story that immerses us in a world of paranoia, confused loyalties, and imminent madness.

2. It is a difficult connection to pinpoint, but clearly the narrator's sense of her own identity—as a female and as a daughter—is uncertain, and her feelings for her father are contradictory. She also seems to be "caught," not just between her mother and father but between their prejudices about what women are and how they should behave. Whether she actually murders her father or not is in some sense irrelevant, for she clearly wants to escape from his power, and her murder fantasy, which may be more than just a fantasy, expresses that desire.

3. Part of the seeming inevitability of the father's murder springs from the fact that people naturally hate him because of his arrogant power. Oates also depicts him as expressing a particular kind of American power—one that is self-centered, arbitrary, and destructive. The father is an overwhelmingly powerful force in his daughter's private life and in the public life he dominates.

4. She has the murder occur, then tells us (via the narrator) that it didn't occur, and then begins a plot that appears to lead back to the original murder scene. Ironically, she effectively uses confusion about the murder to make murder seem fated to happen.

5. This is unclear, and deliberately so. It may be fantasy, it may not. The woman the daughter sees may be herself, or may not. Confusion is part of the point of the story.

6. Physically and emotionally, she is out of place, dominated by her parents, fearing and needing them, obsessed with her father's presence, particularly on television. She is not loved, and her behavior and obsessions seem to spring from a need to be loved and a rage at not being loved.

Luisa Valenzuela, "The Censors"

1. The story has the brevity and streamlined quality of a fairy tale. There is little or no traditional "character development"; the narrator speaks of Juan and Mariana as if we knew them. The plot moves very rapidly, and Juan is driven pell-mell to the ironic twists at the end. Nearly everything except the essential action—and the knowing voice of the narrator—has been discarded.

2. It seems to suggest a certain seductiveness about the power to censor or otherwise control others.

3. One might argue that the story is an intriguing blend of the comic and ridiculous with the deadly seriousness of power (censorship, execution).

4. This particular predicament—and its rapidity—may not be literally acceptable, but its figurative applications certainly are.

5. You might begin by giving a brief working definition of "parable" (one appears in the glossary) and then discuss Biblical and Buddhist parables—their form and purpose. The plot of "The Censors" certainly seems "exemplary" in the sense a parable is.

Richard Brautigan, "The Ghost Children of Tacoma"

1. The story seems to suggest that children are remarkably conscious about the surface details of war—the names of planes, the lingo, etc.—even if the horror of war escapes them (when their country is not under direct attack, that is). He captures the frivolity of the play without moralizing about it.

2. It is light and tongue-in-cheek, rather more like that of a wry autobiographical essay than that of a traditional short story.

3. Brautigan's story is more like a reminiscence than is Valenzuela's, which draws on a classic parable form. Plot dominates Valenzuela's, whereas a catalogue of autobiographical detail dominates Brautigan's.

4. This asks for the students' opinions.

5. They add to the tongue-in-cheek quality because the narrator is so precise about something that is entirely imaginary, and so he captures the detailed quality of children's games of pretend.

Shirley Jackson, "The Lottery"

1. She uses the most basic technique of withholding crucial information; the event for which people are gathering could be any harmless community ritual, but we keep reading because we know there's more to it.

2. This asks for the students' conjecture.

3. The story suggests some of the mindlessness with which people will participate in rituals or other communal efforts. Ironically, these townspeople are critical of the details of the ritual (they substitute paper for wood chips), but they are unconscious of its brutality, and they are unreflective about why they participate. They are very much herd animals, even when the lottery strikes their own family.

4. Many readers quickly forget about the second lottery involving the Hutchinson family, but here the lottery becomes even more brutal, setting family members against one another. Giving the young boy pebbles suggests an initiation of sorts—one that isn't spared even though he will throw them at his mother and at least symbolically participate in her murder.

Alice Walker, "Everyday Use"

1. There are several key conflicts: between the narrator and her elder daughter (their views of life); in a larger sense, between generations in general; between urban and rural worldviews; and between two views of Afro-American culture.

2. It lets us know how commonsensical she is, and how she defines herself in opposition to so-called "mainstream" culture as reflected by television. It also anticipates the conflict between her earthy view of life and her daughter's more pretentious view. In a sense she already knows how the reunion will turn out.

3. The elder daughter behaves like a tourist in her own former home. The mother reacts satirically—making fun of the new names, lacing her narrative with sarcasm.

4. The quilt symbolizes two completely different views of one part of Afro-American culture. To the mother and Maggie, it is first a quilt with a specific practical purpose, and second a "text" of matriarchal knowledge passed from generation to generation. The elder daughter has objectified the quilt, turned it into an art object with no "everyday use" and no local or filial history.

Amos Oz, "If There Is Justice"

1. In both subtle and explicit ways, these descriptions show us how much he has changed, and the statement about his mother's face emerging indicates that any physcial changes are only symptoms of changes in Rami's character.

2. She does not listen well to Rami, she treats him like a child, and she is a bit of a cliché mother in the way she hovers.

3. He seems calm and reflective at first, but the movement or plot of the story drives him into deep despair and doubt.

4. After completing the deadly game, Rami examines his own character, decides what strengths he possesses, and forgives himself for not being a hero. He judges himself by different standards, more realistic ones, perhaps.

Raymond Carver, "Errand"

1. The style early on is journalistic, deliberately "objective" and the furthest thing from sentimental. As the story proceeds, it becomes less reportorial and more dramatic.

2. He is a vivid, eccentric figure in the story. Like his fiction, Tolstoy is a bit grandiose and overblown here, particularly in contrast to Chekhov (and Chekhov's fiction). He adds a touch of comedy, too, with his theatrical entrance and his lecture about immortality.

3. It is memorable in a Chekhovian way because it is slightly absurd and comic, but also touching. The drinking of the champagne is at once silly and appropriate, and there is no direct confrontation with the fact that he is about to die—except, of course, when Chekhov himself comments on the impracticality of ordering oxygen.

4. The young man is befuddled, earnest, sweet, and distracted, and he represents the mundane "life as usual" that we often see in Chekhov's stories. Many of Chekhov's stories feature persons suffering in solitude; their suffering seems to have no effect on the rest of the world. Carver's depiction of Chekhov's death—and his use of the young man—captures this element of Chekhov's fiction.

Part Four: Emerging Voices

Louise Erdrich, "Snares"

1. The narrator is wry, crafty, compassionate, and earthy. He is fairly easygoing, certainly reflective, but not above mischief and certain kinds of revenge. His approach to people seems to be to outthink them.

2. His relationship with Father Damien is friendly but a bit guarded. It's clear that the narrator isn't the orthodox Catholic the father might want him to be, but he seems to go along with Father Damien to humor him.

3. It reveals methods of revenge that are both violent and symbolic, merciful and merciless, spiritual and physical.

4. They don't want to give up the land because once it's gone, it's gone forever.

Keri Hulme, "One Whale, Singing"

1. The deck is a bit stacked. Personally and professionally, the scientist here is rigid and obnoxious, but he does represent one scientific perspective on animal intelligence.

2. The point of view is certainly memorable and vivid, owing to the imagery and the knowledge of what else is in the whale's environment. Some readers may find that the point of view drifts toward sentimentality. Others may ask, "How do we know how accurate it is?" It's certainly a risk worth taking, and a risk worth reading about.

3. It's a perfectly awful relationship, so much so that one wonders how these two ended up with one another. He is so domineering that she is filled with rage. She probably doesn't engage him more because she has given up and is content to let him talk on, virtually to himself.

4. The poetic justice may be too poetic, too contrived, but it's in keeping with the risky, bold nature of the story idea and Hulme's approach to the material.

Sue Grafton, "She Never Came Home"

1. Millhone seems very contemporary, and extremely "laid-back" in contrast to Holmes and Marlowe. She's not the obsessive intellectual Holmes is, and she's not the violent, physical, hard-boiled type that Marlowe is. Like Marlowe, though, she's a cynical loner. In this story, at least, she's quiet, clever, and unobtrusive—accumulating information, threatening no one. One might argue that this adds a genuine feminist (not "feminine") touch to the classic private eye. She does not rely on violence, verbal or physical, and she seems adept at getting information from the office workers, all of whom happen to be women. The male co-worker, the police, and the murderer all seem dim by comparison.

3. Much to her own surprise, she cares about him and tries to comfort him. He makes no attempt to escape or to deny he did it.

4. The first two paragraphs set the place and give us the basic details about the private eye.

Susan Engberg, "A Daughter's Heart"

1. The leanness of her father surprises her, and "it seemed there used to be more of him" hints at the theme of "diminishment" that runs throughout the story.

2. They are a close-knit, friendly, warm, middle-class family, and they greet her with love.

3. At that moment many things coalesce in the story; she is aware more than ever of how much her family has given her (monetarily, emotionally, chronologically), of their frailty, of her powerlessness to halt their frailty. She is becoming intensely aware of change and loss.

4. Ironically, the nap seems to have allowed her mind to relax and respond to the grieving she has been doing under the surface of her awareness. The nap seems to have given her the energy to grieve, and she finally responds to the troubling images and thoughts that have been running through her mind. The story is very subtle, very gradual, and some readers may feel that not enough has happened for her to cry; on the other hand, the clues of her new awareness are everywhere.

Jayne Anne Phillips, "Bess"

1. The narrator suggests that it was summer she should have feared, not winter.

2. Terror is mixed with awe. In a way, it turns their sibling relationship into a kind of marriage, as if the relationship had been obliquely and indirectly consummated. Voyeurism runs throughout the story: later Bess secretly watches Warwick walk the highwire, and even the parade scene features a form of "secret watching" on the part of Bess.

3. That summer Bess is overwhelmed by knowledge of sex, guilt, and love. Her relationship with Warwick is transformed into something extraordinary, and he has a hold on her the rest of her life.

4. The voyeurism connects several of the scenes, and of course the powerful figure of Warwick runs throughout them. Phillips is also good at creating an oppressive atmosphere in almost every scene—a kind of correlative to Bess' having said "I understood too much."

Matt Ellison, "Civil Engineer"

1. He's impressionable and naive. He's also fairly "ordinary" insofar as he hates Spanish rice and sees the town and his parents through innocent eyes.

2. It's very much "small-town America," with gossip, petty competitions, small churches, and tract houses. Eric, of course, does not view it this way; he has a rather magical view of his own hometown.

3. Eric's mother is all for Donny Sederholm—until he charges for his professinal services. Eric believes he is to blame for the bill and the subsequent falling out. Eric's mother laments that architects can't make a living—while refusing to treat Donny professionally.

4. It's funny and poignant. It also signals growth and loss of innocence on Eric's part. In a way, his daydream is an elegy for a town he can never know, a town he believes he once lived in. In this sense, "blueprints" symbolize his innocent aspirations for a perfect world.

Elsa Joubert, "Back Yard"

1. This asks for the students' responses, but one might suggest that the narrator gives us a sense that the people who work for her have erected numerous barriers—in language, interaction, behavior—so that even when she thinks she is "communicating" with them, she is not. One might also argue, though, that she is being a bit disingenuous —that she does understand the "existence" of these people and the causes of it.

2. She seems either to fear or pity them.

3. Because she is white, she has social and political power of the people she works for; she is "sanctioned" by apartheid. She is powerless insofar as these Black women do not trust her, do not allow her into their world.

4. The tone here is restrained—tight-lipped, careful, cool. Having said she does not understand the existence of those on whose periphery she lives, she proceeds tentatively to explain herself, step by step, almost as if she were afraid to say too much.

5. This asks for the students' explanations of what they felt they learned about South Africa.

Liliana Heker, "The Stolen Party"

1. By winning the argument about "the monkey," Rosaura believes she is right about the whole party, and the issues her mother raises about why Rosaura was invited, and whether rich people are fair and nice. The opening sets up Rosaura for her disillusionment.

2. The interrogation reinforces what the mother said, but it also shows that the children Rosaura's age also are aware of—and enforce —differences in social classes.

3. She does not receive a gift because she was invited there as an employee, not as a friend.

4. She receives money because she has been employed. The difference in class is driven home mercilessly. She seems to age years in one moment.

5. This last image provides a surprising and effective ending that suggests deep animosity, huge differences between classes, and also the hint of a balance (or imbalance) altered.

Richard Cortez Day, "A Chagall Story"

1. It is not at all what he expected: life goes on without him—and quite soon after he dies. His religious assumptions are incorrect, his sense of how his family will react is wrong, and the questions he asks are inappropriate. But at the end of his flight through and over Florence, his perception of the city—and of his life—is full of light, spirit, and beauty.

2. He discovers that his preconceived notions are wrong, that his family (at least some of them) are greedy, that his friends forget him quickly, and that his city remains the Florence that he knew—only more so.

3. The answer depends on one's perspective, of course. It might be unwise to rush to the conclusion that the conversation is sacrilegious because one real outcome of it is that Guido learns he is applying mortal notions to immortal things, and this is not an essentially sacrilegious "lesson." The conversation is funny, ironic, and therefore far from pious, however.

4. He seems to mean that Guido is rather dogged in applying notions of time, space, a traditional heaven, etc., to a spiritual world that is rather spiritual: unpredictable, jumbled, untethered to earthly concerns.

5. The ending is suggestive, not precise or dogmatic, but it seems to hint that Guido has accepted his death and his new life, and that the new life is all about seeing his city afresh. Many readers may get a generous, whimsical feeling from Day's resolution to Guido's tale.

6. The students will draw their own conclusions, of course, but the story certainly is full of the light, the whimsy, and the poignancy of much of Chagall's work, particularly some of his stained-glass creations.

Shawn Hsu Wong, "Each Year Grain"

1. Aside from allowing the narrator to travel back in time, the opening paragraph also establishes the firm connection between land and history that the story explores. The joys and agonies of the story are deeply connected to the landscape, and the tree therefore becomes an excellent metaphor for the history that has grown out of that land.

2. One might say that the language in these sections is more "poetic" —heightened, compressed, highly imagistic. The grandfather (as a young boy) seems to speak the first one; the next three seem to be spoken by a separate narrator, or to "stand alone," as it were, as poems of the land. These sections enrich the story and add texture to the more traditional narration.

3. It is a complicated relationship. He is often awed by the beauty, but then the land almost becomes an accomplice to what has happened to the Chinese, as evidenced by the wish of so many of them to have their remains returned to China.

4. They were brought—or "invited"—to California to help build the railroads, but they were essentially an exploited work force, treated badly when they were building the railroad, paid relatively nothing, and then subjected to deeply racist laws and fierce xenophobia.

5. The story celebrates the land, and it also celebrates one racial and cultural group who became Californians and Americans. It indicts a particularly ugly racist and exploitative episode of California and American history.

Rick Demarinis, "Under the Wheat"

1. The story seems deliberately episodic, presenting scenes in a kind of collage form, without a conventional sense of continuity or transition but still with a cumulative power, a sense of "things getting worse." It is in this latter sense that the story has a traditional plot, or at least a movement toward crisis, toward the action at its most intense. The conflict is really the alienation that haunts the narrator.

2. The general time period is suggested by many references, but the narrator actually gives the date of July 15, 1962, at one point.

3. The students will say which ones are most vivid in their minds, but there are constant references to firing the missiles, to accidents, mishaps, and malfunctions.

4. He seems aimless and often dull-witted, robotic at times. But probably no one would call him malevolent; he is banal, indifferent —and therefore all the more chilling for being in charge of missiles.

Stephen King, "Graveyard Shift"

1. Here are a few key elements: an unsuspecting victim, darkness, a monstrosity, violence, graphic detail, and a situation that exploits universal human fears.

2. The time (night) and the place (an isolated workplace with a region "down below") seem crucial to King's purposes.

3. They are fairly ordinary, unsuspecting characters who underestimate the monstrosity.

4. This asks for the students' opinions, but one could at least argue that King's descriptions are precise and graphic.

Tess Gallaghar, "A Pair of Glasses"

1. The glasses seem important to her because adults wear glasses, because she feels different wearing them, and because they become for her a kind of mask that represents a different identity. Later in the story, when they become more of an issue, involving her teacher and parents, they resonate evan more with symbolic power, and they mark a coming-of-age point in her life.

2. They do not understand her wall at all, least of all when they behave as if they do understand. They patronize her.

3. It's an interesting narrative strategy that places the story in a domain that is not quite third person and not quite first person. The narrative point of view is certainly sympathetic to the girl, but the term "the girl" also creates a certain distance or coolness.

4. The girl takes a more bitter, more cynical look at the world after the teacher removes the glasses from the rims; she learns about dishonesty and manipulation.

Alberto Alvaro Rios, "The Iguana Killer"

1. This asks for the students' opinions of what is "exotic" about the story. One way to rephrase the question in class is to ask the ways in which Sapito is a "universal" boy and in what ways he seems shaped by his culture, his town, his family, his own personality.

2. Snow is a completely new experience for him, almost magical. Having this new experience gives him a sense of being different or having a kind of power, and this sense may lead him to fabricate.

3. He's a curious, bright person—mischievous in some ways, innocent in some ways, kind in some ways—and, at least from the iguana's point of view, brutal in some ways.

4. He kills iguanas without much thought; this may alienate some readers, but his motivation in making a crib seams generous, even selfless.

5. It is a time when Sapito is becoming aware of a larger world, both in geographical and social terms. He is becoming aware of his niche in the world.

Njabulo Ndebele, "Death of a Son"

1. The narrator reports that to some extent, the death has brought them closer together.

2. The death and the circumstances surrounding it show how dehumanizing the regime in South Africa can be. It also shows how complete and arbitrary the government's power is over Black citizens, and it shows how powerless these citizens sometimes feel. It also shows the rage and frustration that they feel.

3. At least, in this story, the women tend to band together more, to grieve together. To a degree, they also seem more resilient, better able to deal with frustration and rage. It's revealing that the narrator's statements privilege the sharing of concern over revenge.

4. She is stronger, she says, because it is all right for her to be afraid and to then go on and deal with the fear. Because Buntu is not supposed to be afraid, he has to invent ways of hiding that emotion.

5. Much of the imagery at the end of the story is apocalyptic. Her hope springs from her recognition that she and Buntu can have another child, and from her sense that they are more resilient than even they at first had realized.

Fiona Barr, "The Wall-Reader"

1. It is a dangerous, bleak place, where she nonetheless finds "pockets" of solitude and peace.

2. It depersonalizes him and shows how she is forced to think of him not as a person but as a "force" or a symbol of political power.

3. The "voice" is a British soldier; the narrator is a Catholic. Therefore, each is on the opposite side of the political conflict. The Provisional Irish Republican Army discourages Catholic citizens from having anything to do with British soldiers, and so the narrator is treated as a traitor when she is discovered talking to the soldier.

4. The Provos are the Provisional Irish Republican Army, a kind of police force representing one segment of the Catholic community in Northern Ireland, particularly Belfast. The wall divides the Catholic and Protestant neighborhoods in Belfast; it used to be a series of houses, many of which were torn down and replaced by a genuine wall.

Sesshu Foster, "The Street of the Fathers"

1. The narrator suggests that the fathers and their alcoholism broke each family apart and also caused the young woman to move.

2. He is thoughtful and reflective, and responds in a curiously accepting way to being beaten up on his graduation night. He grows into a successful person who nonetheless longs for the neighborhood and for the young woman with whom he was infatuated.

3. In part she seems to represent a particularly passionate, hopeful time in his life, and she seems also to represent a time in his life that was somehow more "real" than the corporate life he leads now.

4. The dream is poignant because it unites him with his father and because it recapitulates the stunted romance with the young woman. The last image is one of industrial sterility; the crane suggests the depersonalized world in which he now lives.

James Welch, "Fools Crow"

1. Fools Crow is certainly the central forceful personality in the story, but the multiple points of view make it more than "his" story, and they illuminate the emotions and ideas of many characters.

2. In many ways the point of view of the children is universal. They are jealous and flirtatious, cruel and friendly. What they are doing and where they are doing it, though, are particular to Native American culture.

3. It is probably rabies.

4. We find out a lot about their way of life—where they get food, how they treat illnesses, how spirituality informs their daily life, how women and men function together, and what young girls and boys aspire to.

5. In a wry way, the narrator lets us know that One Spot has been cured.

Guyan Ranjan, "Our Side of the Fence and Theirs"

1. He is very suspicious, watchful, and prejudiced.

2. Chiefly, they offend him by being different, not by being intrusive. Even the fact that they don't play a radio troubles him, for instance, even though it would seem to be an inoffensive difference.

3. The story suggests that conflict is embedded in perception and prejudice, and that open conflict often emerges from suspicion, ignorance, and paranoia.

4. The story suggests that many Indian families are extended ones and that they represent a complicated social structure in and of themselves.

Madeline DeFrees, "The Ventriloquist's Dummy"

1. She is eccentric and earnest, with firmly established ideas and habits. She is not sophisticated, but she is curiously "aware." She is often unintentionally funny.

2. We find out that, essentially, she thinks everyone is a criminal and that her search for the Green River Killer is really a search for a violent or asocial element in everyone. The ending makes it clear that she almost has a desire to be a victim, and that nearly being a victim liberates her, oddly enough.

3. In part she fantasizes about being famous, and in part she has a morbid interest in crime.

4. The end of the story reinforces the theme of complicity, and it plays out, in a ritual way, the violence that Frieda fears and that also fascinates her.

Martin Amis, "Bujack and the Strong Force"

1. It's certainly a *considered* analogy, whether it works well for all readers or not. Bujack lives by force and as much as any person is tempted to exact revenge, so the choice is a powerful one for him, and Amis takes pains to weave the choice into a context of nuclear warfare.

2. Each of these groups has been the victim of genocide in the twentieth century.

3. Each man brings his personal temperament and background to bear on the argument for or against revenge, and we know from the outset that Bujack is the man of "strong force," while the narrator is passive, nonviolent, reflective, wary—not a man of action or reaction.

4. He connects Einsteinian physics, nuclear war, and historical references to the "everyday" part of the story fairly straightforwardly, and the kind of narrator he uses—a knowledgeable person unafraid of these ideas—makes the connection believable, or at least acceptable *if* readers accept the voice and perspective of the narrator. "Connects" may be mistating the method Amis uses because, in a sense, the story aims to show that these larger contexts of physics, war, and history are fully a part of "everyday life."